This book is dedicated to
Tony Kenneth Pinder

# OXFORD
## UNIVERSITY PRESS

Great Clarendon Street, Oxford OX2 6DP

Oxford University Press is a department of the University of Oxford.
It furthers the University's objective of excellence in research, scholarship,
and education by publishing worldwide in

Oxford  New York

Athens  Auckland  Bangkok  Bogotá  Buenos Aires  Calcutta
Cape Town  Chennai  Dar es Salaam  Delhi  Florence  Hong Kong  Istanbul
Karachi  Kuala Lumpur  Madrid  Melbourne  Mexico City  Mumbai
Nairobi  Paris  São Paulo  Singapore  Taipei  Tokyo  Toronto  Warsaw

with associated companies in  Berlin  Ibadan

Oxford is a registered trade mark of Oxford University Press
in the UK and in certain other countries

British Library Cataloguing in Publication Data available

ISBN 0–19–279042–0 (hardback)
ISBN 0–19–272381–2 (paperback)

Printed in China

ARTHUR CONAN DOYLE'S

# THE HOUND OF THE BASKERVILLES

ADAPTED AND ILLUSTRATED BY

## CHRIS MOULD

# THE CURSE

My good friend Mr Sherlock Holmes and I were seated at the breakfast table. Though we did not know it, a great mystery was already heading to our door, which only the genius of Holmes, (a specialist in crime), could unravel.

'When the late Hugo Baskerville, of evil reputation, held the manor in the late seventeenth century he had come to love a young maiden nearby. In anger at her rejection of him he stole away with her on his horse one night.

The arrival of Dr Mortimer was of no surprise to us. He had called earlier and we expected his return.

'Mr Holmes, Dr Watson, I am pleased to meet you,' he said.

'And how may we help you?' enquired Holmes.

'I have a manuscript,' he said, taking a paper from his pocket. 'It was put into my care by Sir Charles Baskerville of Devonshire who has recently died. It is about a certain legend which runs in the family. With your permission, sir, I will read it to you.' And he began the story:

'She was locked up in the Hall, but she managed to escape. When he found she had fled he went out across the moonlit moor to search for her. His men followed behind and eventually they came across their bodies. To their horror a great black beast of a hound with blazing eyes and dripping jaws stood over them.

'Such is the legend of the Baskervilles. Now the details surrounding Sir Charles's death have not been satisfactorily explained. He was found outside at night. He was not marked and his heart was known to be weak, but something else bothers me. When I examined the ground nearby I found the footprints of a large hound.'

'There have been many sightings on the moor of a large creature, ghastly, with burning eyes and a mouth of fire. Today the heir, Sir Henry Baskerville, arrives from America. I fear for his safety. I must have your help.'

The following morning Dr Mortimer returned, accompanied by Sir Henry who gave to Holmes a letter he had received on his arrival. It warned him away from the moor.

'Is there anything else?' asked Holmes.

'Well, I left a pair of boots outside my door last night. I awoke this morning to find that one was missing.'

'Strange,' said Holmes scratching his forehead. He decided to relate the Baskerville legend to Sir Henry.

Even so, Sir Henry was adamant that he would go to his family home. He suggested we should meet later at his hotel when he had had a chance to think things through.

As they left, Holmes turned to me. 'Your coat and hat, Dr Watson, quickly.' And we followed the two of them at a safe distance in the hope that we might learn something.

Suddenly we noticed a cab on the road doing the same. A bearded man looked keenly after them and then he saw us. In a flash the cab was off. Holmes tried to follow, but to no avail.

'At least I have the cab number,' said Holmes, although by this time we had also lost Dr Mortimer and Sir Henry.

# BASKERVILLE HALL

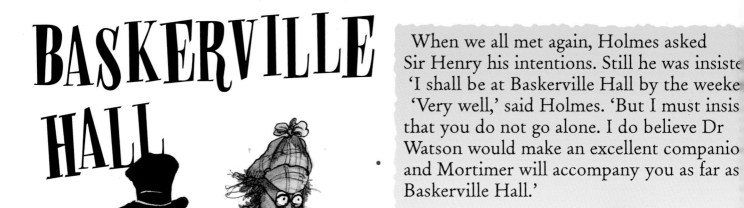

When we all met again, Holmes asked Sir Henry his intentions. Still he was insiste 'I shall be at Baskerville Hall by the weeke 'Very well,' said Holmes. 'But I must insis that you do not go alone. I do believe Dr Watson would make an excellent companio and Mortimer will accompany you as far as Baskerville Hall.'

I made arrangements for my journey.

In the meantime Holmes had caught up with the cab driver who insisted that his passenger had given his name as—Mr Sherlock Holmes.

The journey to Dartmoor was swift and pleasant. In a short time the city of London had turned into the rolling hills of Devon. When we left our train, a carriage awaited us. Turning a corner we came across an armed policeman on a horse, his rifle held up on his arm.

'What is this?' cried Mortimer.

'There's a convict escaped from the prison, sir,' said our driver. 'It's Selden, sir, the Notting Hill murderer.'
The road ahead grew bleaker and wilder. Huge oaks and firs twisted by years of storms surrounded us and then two turrets rose up above. The driver pointed with his whip. 'Baskerville Hall, sir.'
Soon we were passing through the huge gates and along the driveway up to the house. A tall figure appeared from the porch in the darkness.

Another figure appeared. The two were Mr and Mrs Barrymore, the butler and housekeeper.
'Welcome to Baskerville Hall, Sir Henry.'
Dr Mortimer said goodbye and took the carriage to his home nearby.

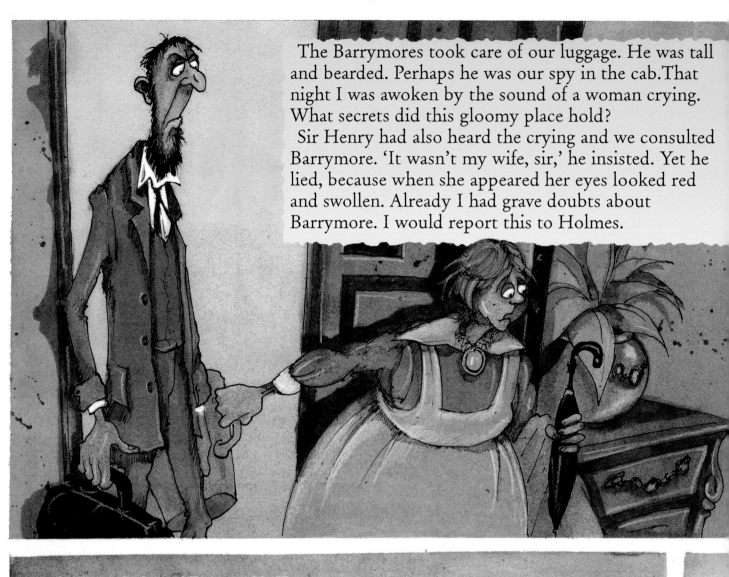

The Barrymores took care of our luggage. He was tall and bearded. Perhaps he was our spy in the cab. That night I was awoken by the sound of a woman crying. What secrets did this gloomy place hold?

Sir Henry had also heard the crying and we consulted Barrymore. 'It wasn't my wife, sir,' he insisted. Yet he lied, because when she appeared her eyes looked red and swollen. Already I had grave doubts about Barrymore. I would report this to Holmes.

'We were sorry about Sir Charles,' he continued. 'Do you know the legend of the hound?'

Again I heard of the fiendish dog that haunted Dartmoor. Just then a low moan swept across the moor. 'Hear that?' he asked. 'Some say it is the cry of the hound. Strange place, the moor.'

Suddenly he was distracted with a butterfly and began chasing around with his net.

After breakfast I took the opportunity to get to know the moor. A voice called me, introducing itself. 'I am Stapleton of Merripit House, I live nearby.' I had heard of Stapleton, a local naturalist.

The sound of footsteps drew near and I turned to greet a handsome woman. This was the sister of my acquaintance. 'Go back,' she cried. 'Go back to London immediately. Keep away from here.'

I could only stare in surprise at her greeting. As it turned out she had taken me to be Sir Henry, but even so, I could not understand her attitude. Later she apologized to me but could not explain her words. Only that this place was one of danger.

# DEAR HOLMES

Dear Holmes . . .

It is like another world out here on the moor. It is a vast place yet it is charming. Let me return now to the facts. We have not heard or seen anything of the escaped prisoner. He could easily hide out here but there is no way he could obtain food. My guess is that he has moved on.

Mr Barrymore also intrigues me and I must tell you a further mystery. I was awoken again in the night. Footsteps passed my room and I looked through my door. It was Barrymore. He carried a candle and passed down the corridor into an empty room.

There seems to be a mutual attraction between Sir Henry and Miss Stapleton. The Stapletons dine here tonight and there is talk of us going to Merripit House. One would imagine that this match would be welcome to Stapleton but I somehow feel that he disapproves.

Mrs Barrymore interests me. I told you of her sobbing in the night. I am convinced she's hiding some secret sorrow.

I watched him further. He crouched at the window and held the candle close to the glass as he stared out across the moor. After some time he put out the light and I made haste back to my room. Again his footsteps came past my door. There is some secret business going on here. I have spoken to Sir Henry and we have made plans to deal with the matter. I shall write again when there is more to tell you.

Watson

Baskerville Hall
15th October

Dear Holmes . . .

Today I found myself in a
most awkward position. Sir
Henry put on his coat and
prepared to go out. I did the
same but it was clear that a
meeting with Miss Stapleton
was Sir Henry's reason for a
walk on the moor. I did not
wish to leave him alone and
followed at a safe distance.

Soon I realized I was not the
only onlooker. Stapleton's
butterfly net caught my eye.
He was approaching fast and
there was some kind of
quarrel between the three of
them. What all this was about
I could not tell.

I caught up with Sir Henry as he wandered
back to Baskerville Hall looking dejected.
With a heavy heart he explained to me how
he had asked Miss Stapleton to marry him.
Stapleton had heard and had lost his temper.
We were both puzzled but our confusion was
answered when Stapleton arrived in the
afternoon to apologize.

'I am sorry,' he pleaded, 'but my sister is all
I have out here. I did not mean to be rude.'

And by way of an apology we were invited
to dine at Merripit House on the following
Friday. Sir Henry has decided not to pursue
the relationship for now.

The Barrymore mystery I am pleased to say is cleared up. Sir Henry and I found Barrymore at the window as before and confronted him. Mrs Barrymore appeared and together they explained.

The escaped convict is Mrs Barrymore's brother. The candle was a signal to let him know there was food for him.

'He has the reputation of an evil man, but to me he will always be the small boy who I nursed.' And she wept as she spoke.

Sir Henry and I decided to go in search of Selden and as we stood out on the moor we heard again the distant howl. We could only catch a glimpse of Selden, who was away quickly. But the strangest thing is that I swear I saw another tall dark figure while I was out on the moor.

Watson

It was decided to let Selden slip out of sight, and in his gratitude Barrymore came forward with information which he thought might be of help. 'Perhaps I should have mentioned it before, sir,' he whispered to Sir Henry, 'but it was a long time afterwards that I found out.'

'What is it, Barrymore?'
'When Sir Charles met his death that night he was there to meet a woman, sir. My wife found the remains of a letter in the fire, sir. It said, "Please, as you are a gentleman, burn this letter and be at the gate by ten o'clock. Signed L.L."'
If I could discover the identity of L.L. we would be somewhat nearer a solution.

In the evening I put on my coat and walked out upon the moor. After some time Dr Mortimer came by in his carriage and gave me a lift back to the Hall.
'By the way,' I asked, 'do you know of any person with the initials L.L.?'
'Well, yes, there is Miss Laura Lyons of Coombe Tracey.'
I decided to seek out this woman. I spoke with Barrymore. He too knew of another man upon the moor. Selden had spoken of him but had not known his identity. When would we solve this tangled web of mysteries?

The following day I had to establish two important facts concerning the death of Sir Charles. Laura Lyons of Coombe Tracey had written to him and made an appointment to see him at the time of his death. Also, I had to seek out the man lurking on the moor. His presence was too much of a mystery to be ignored.

I searched every corner of the barren moor. In a cleft of the hills I discovered a circle of stone huts. One was in good repair. Perhaps my man was inside. I crept in. It was empty but the ashes of a recent fire smouldered silently.

Suddenly, I heard him. Footsteps drew near. I shrank into the corner, my pistol cocked inside my pocket. A shadow fell across the opening.

When I reached Coombe Tracey I found Miss Lyons at work in her office. I had difficulty discovering the truth about her meeting with Sir Charles. She was adamant that in the end she did not keep her appointment. She had meant to go to him to ask for financial help but when she received it from someone else she did not turn up. I felt that she was keeping something back from me.

As I drove back to the Hall I looked out across the landscape which had become so familiar to me.

'It is a lovely evening, Watson,' came a familiar voice.

'Holmes,' I said, and he stood there before me with a wry smile and his pipe smoking in his mouth.

I was never so glad to see anyone as I was to see Holmes just then. But why was he out here?

'My dear fellow, I have been secretly following the investigation from here alone, not to deceive you but because I could not have made the discoveries I have made while living at Baskerville Hall. I was merely looking at the investigation from a different point of view. My own findings tell me that a close intimacy exists between our friend Stapleton and Miss Lyons and the lady he passes off as his sister is actually his wife.'

'What?' I cried. Suddenly his objections to Sir Henry became clear. 'But why the deception?' All our suspicions began to descend on our friend the naturalist.

'Stapleton saw that his wife would be more useful to his murderous plans in the guise of a single woman,' said Holmes. 'Was it he, disguised, who dogged us in London?' I asked. 'I believe so,' he answered. 'Our nets are closing in on him and soon we will have him.'

Suddenly an awful scream filled the air. We sprang to our feet. It was followed by that awful sound which I knew to be the hound. We searched high and low and eventually we found a twisted broken body at the foot of a slope. The unmistakable red tweed coat of Sir Henry's lay upon its back.

We approached the body only to find it was not Sir Henry, it was Holmes's neighbour, the convict. I remembered how Sir Henry had passed on his old clothes to Barrymore, who must have passed them on to Selden.

Stapleton had heard the cries and appeared on the scene. It was clear to us that he hid some disappointment that it was not Sir Henry.

Back at the Hall Sir Henry was greatly pleased to see Holmes. First we had to break the news of Selden's death to the Barrymores. She wept bitterly but I think that really he was relieved.

'How is the enquiry coming along?' questioned Sir Henry.

'It is a baffling mystery,' admitted Holmes, 'but we are getting there.'

Later, Holmes was admiring Baskerville Hall and looking intently at the portraits.

'Aaah, the very wicked Hugo,' he said, stopping at one.

Later, in darkness, he led me back, holding a candle to it. 'Notice anything?' he asked and suddenly the face of Stapleton sprang out at me. Another missing link. Was Stapleton really a Baskerville with a keen eye on the manor?

The following morning we told Sir Henry that Holmes and I were to go to London. 'Please apologize to the Stapletons for us and explain that we cannot dine with them tonight but that you will go along on your own. Make sure that you walk home. Now, Watson,' he continued, taking me to one side, 'we must visit Laura Lyons.'

Holmes was frank. 'You asked Sir Charles to be at his gate at ten o'clock. This was the time and place of his death.'
When Holmes told her that Stapleton's supposed sister was his wife she decided to reveal all.
Stapleton had dictated the letter requesting the meeting. He then dissuaded her from keeping the appointment. This ensured that he would be out at night all alone.

I now learned that we were not to return to London but it should only appear so. Soon we were back on the road to Merripit House.

Holmes stopped about a hundred yards from the house where we could be screened by a mound of rocks. A dense fog loomed in the distance.

We fired our pistols together. The beast yelped out in pain and then fell to the ground. It was dead. Sir Henry was shocked but not hurt. We looked at the hound. Phosphorous covered the open mouth. 'Trickery,' said Holmes.

Eventually, after much waiting, Sir Henry left the house for the walk home. The fog closed in. Suddenly, we were struck motionless as a huge hound sprang from the shadows of the mist. Fire burst from its mouth, its eyes glowed. Never had we seen anything so demonic.

We returned to Merripit House. Our man had fled, but on searching the house we found his wife restrained in an upstairs room.
'Where has he gone?' asked Holmes.

'There is a tin mine upon the moor, surrounded by a huge bog, the Grimpen Mire. It is there he kept the beast.'
But he could not have found his way through the fog that night. The next day we searched the Mire and found the last traces of Stapleton. A boot stuck out of the mud. It was Sir Henry's missing boot; Stapleton had used it to give the dog the scent of his victim.

We were back in Baker Street by a blazing fire and Dartmoor was a distant memory. There was still much, though, that I did not have clear in my mind. Holmes explained.

'Stapleton was indeed a Baskerville, though a long-lost one. Because of his previous involvement in criminal activity he had changed his identity. He had kept a keen eye on Baskerville Hall and had discovered that only two lives lay between himself and a large estate.

'Sir Charles had told him of the legend and so had given him the very idea in the first place. He bought a huge dog and kept it upon the moor. When he lured Sir Charles outside at night Stapleton set the dog at him with phosphorus blazing like fire from its jaws. This finished his already weakened heart.

'Stapleton had decided he might be able to do away with Sir Henry in London, hence the disguise. He needed something to set the dog upon his track and so the mystery of the missing boot was born. The warning note was from Mrs Stapleton, fearful of her husband's intentions.

'I stayed on the moor to watch Stapleton. Selden's death was an attempt on Sir Henry's life.

'We had to catch him red-handed, hence our action at dinner that night.'

'How then would he have claimed Baskerville Hall without being known to be a Baskerville?' I asked.

'That, my friend, is something I cannot tell you. One thing is certain, our man was never short of ideas. And now, my dear Watson, I feel we have done enough work for one day. Grab your coat, sir, we shall take an evening stroll and discuss tomorrow.'